THE YOLK and other stories
by David Backer

"The Yolk," "The Jewelry Party," "Mollify," and "In the Land of Tongues" appeared in *Metazen;* "Will#17" appeared in *Caterwaul Quarterly*; "Come and be a part of it!" appeared in *The Delinquent*; "Capitalism" appeared in *Nanoism*; "Bob and Steve Coming Together" appeared in *Sleep.Snort.Fuck*; "Variegated" appeared in *Johnny America*; "Tractable" appeared in *Keyhole Digest, Vol. 1*; "Solicitous" appeared in *Zygote in my Coffee*; "Refractory" appeared in *Curly Red Stories*; "Puerility" appeared in *Emprise Review*; "Proscribe" appeared in *kill author*; "Paucity" appeared in *Daily Love*; "Disinter" appeared *The Locust Review*; "Extrude" appeared in *The Houston Literary Review*; "Select Facestories" appeared as "Eight Facestories" in *Swink Magazine*; "Something in the Ones and Zeros" appeared in *Children, Churches, and Daddies*; "Man Writing Story with Ears Plugged about Painter who Only Hears in Color, Black Ink, 2002" appeared in *Diet Soap*; "Jon and Maeve" appeared in *Forty Stories, A Collection of New Writing*; "Because We're The Impressive" appeared in *STORYCHORD*; "A Manual for Readers" appeared in *Luna Park Review*.

Table of Contents

Flash[1]

---
[1] Stories >1,000 words.

The Yolk

Let me explain it. It's a house of eggs. Built from the ground up. Dozens upon dozens of eggs. There's a base and columns that rest on the base. The columns are two eggs wide, 2×2, supported by the base, which is sixteen eggs wide, to support the columns. I don't know how but there's a roof. A roof of eggs. And it's tall. It gets to be my height. It gets so that people start noticing. "Hey, look at that thing he's building, it's made of eggs." "Yes, it looks very impressive." It gets to the point where I'm proud of it. I want to finish it. So I'm putting a steeple on it, which seems appropriate, or, rather, that's how the house of eggs appears in my mind—with a steeple. I'm putting the steeple on it and there's a crowd. My friends have gathered and they've told their families, who know me, and they've all told their friends, and now it's an event. A happening, my finishing the house of eggs. It's a presentation. I'm wearing a suit and tie. I'm about to put the last egg on top of that steeple and I hear something. I don't know what it is. I don't let it phase me. I'm all about this house of eggs. It's me. Who I've become. People ask me about it. I have a blog and a twitter account. My Facebook picture is a picture of the house of eggs. I have publications devoted to the philosophy and history and economics and anthropology of the house of eggs. I'm called "Mr. House of Eggs" in some circles. It won't, can't fail. If it fails then so do I. So I place the last egg upon the steeple and claps begin. But I hear the sound again. More frequently now. A tick. A crack. The shells are breaking. First the bottom and then throughout, yellow amniotic fluid slithering down the columns. Dripping. The house of eggs is bleeding. Crying. Then the shells, only ever shells, double and fold upon themselves and the house of eggs falls into a soup, chaos, destruction. No one can believe it. Some time passes and people walk away. My friends put their hands on my shoulders but they have lives too and they leave. My family, eventually, does the same. I'm left with the entropic pile of my great failure, myself in shambles, the universe in ruin. The yolk of the eggs creeps toward me. I think of chickens. I think of all the people in the world who just want an omelet. I think: The yolk is on me.

Will #17

I want crazy at my funeral.

I want clowns, a petting zoo, fireworks, craps tables, male and female strippers, and a three-person band composed of old men wearing striped vests, black pants, and straw hats: one plays a banjo, another on tuba, and the lead on clarinet.

I want a popcorn machine, a maypole, a DJ playing the Macarena, the electric slide. He will be giving away prizes. I want a fog machine. I want a Greek chorus wearing plaster tragedy masks. I want my best friends to play each other at air hockey. I want a roller rink and a movie set of fake skyscrapers. I want a Ford Model-T on display there. I want people to dig trenches like they did in World War One. I want a gas chamber that sprays pixy sticks instead of poison.

I want a rabbi, a priest, a Jain, a Sikh, a Chinese villager who prays to Confucian, Taoist, and Buddhist gods. I want Kathy Lee Gifford. I want Stan Getz playing a Bill Evans tune. I want J. Robert Oppenheimer quoting the Bhagavad-Gita on an old-style radio microphone while giving out lollipops and sparklers.

I want Pynchon, Steinbeck, Salinger, Vonnegut, and Joseph Heller and my parents and this guy named Topaz I met on a train once to brainstorm what my epitaph should be. I want there to be a sing along. I want there to be children and those about to die and pregnant mothers and veterans. I want farmers with tractors and pesticides, immigrants loitering and hippies in suits and flip-flops playing Frisbee. I want Nick Drake to give a lecture on the conversational arts. I want every single pair of glasses I've ever had strung up with bat repellant and bunting.

I want Grand Central helicoptered in.

The Jewelry Party

It's a jewelry party. Everyone's invited.

Hoop Earring, hostess, sits at the head of an oak table. She wears bunches of knitted human ears on each end of her metal head. They're petrified now, the ears, from so many parties. Hoop laughs at a joke and the ears click-clack against each other as she turns from side to side admiring her guests.

Next to her sits Chain-link Necklace, erect, skins of human necks weaved through her links. She's Protestant, proper, waspy. She desires Hoops husband, Pinkie Ring–a hand-shaped ring that wears a man's body wrapped around its pinkie finger, the man's arms fastened to his legs adorning the metal hand whose palm, relaxed, faces outwards like Christ's–but Chain-link doesn't dare make a move on Pinkie. Not yet. Not with all the drama. She restricts herself to fantasy and listens to the chatter around her.

Nose Bone, the lesbian punk rocker, sits a few chairs away, garnered in nostrils and sinuses and mucus. She sneezes and excuses herself from the table and walks to the music room, lighting a hand-wrapped cigarette and smoking

it near an open window. Toe Ring sits next to
Nose Bone, wearing a dress of toes (big, pointy,
middle, ring, little). Across from her is Belly Bar
wrapped twice around with a string of navels
(innies, outies). Nipple Horseshoe sits next to
Belly festooned in a dress of aureoles (vestigial,
useful).

And then, yes, of course, the front gate slams.
They all hear it. She's arrived.

Footsteps down the hallway. She appears in the
open door. Clit Fourchette. Small, unexpected,
a wonder to behold. Conversation stops.

She enters the dining room. Bowls of soup,
brought to the guests by Hoops napkin-servants,
steam into their faces from the table. They stare.
They can't–won't–believe it. Clit Fourchette had
an affair with Pinkie less than a year ago,
almost causing divorce, though the regal couple
managed to stay together after many
appointments with a psychiatrist made of
psychotropic pills (green, blue, yellow, white)
and a priest made of the sins of the penitent
(active, lapsed). But here she is, Clit, so elusive,
so essential, so–daring. She wears a tube top
made of labia covered by a long jacket woven
from pubic hair–an Obama for President! button
on the lapel– her warm midriff teasing just
enough to entice.

The party eyes Clit.

Clit eyes the party.

What will betide them?

No one on this Earth knows the future!

Not ever!

As happens frequently in the wealthiest arrangements it's the hostess that moves our story forward. Hoop says to Clit: "You've got some nerve coming here."

In The Land of Tongues

I walked in tongues. A land of them. As far as I could see: tongues. Wet, red, papillated, salivating muscles, iterating in waves, one upon the other. I was alone. The sky, blue. Nearly cloudless. The terrain, flat. Reflecting pink in all directions. My legs were sunk up to my ankles and I stood on a ground the tongues created together. A fundament of tongues. They made licking sounds, crawling but not moving, lapping but not speaking–it was the sound of a constant kiss.

I moved to take a step and the tongues released my foot. They curled away to let me proceed, though I had no destination in mind. When I brought my foot down they allowed it to settle into them again, gently nestling around it, receiving it, holding it in their humid and loose grasp.

There was a moment of calm. Then I heard a noise. A shriek. I turned and saw a black stripe moving through the tongues. It was like a snake or serpent or eel. I heard the noise again. Shrieking. I felt the snake-like thing against my leg, but it wasn't a snake. It felt familiar: synthetic, fabricated.

Suddenly a man's belt sprang out from between the tongues–a brown leather belt, business casual–and it hit me in the teeth with it's metal buckle. I doubled over, covering my mouth, and my front teeth cracked. Blood streamed through my fingers. Another belt, this time a black one, hit me in the eye. I fell into the tongues. More belts came and pulled me into their fundament, dark and fleshy.

What I saw was discomfiting. Where I'd been standing–the land of tongues–was actually the top of some roof, or the underside of some floor, I couldn't tell which. On the other side were lines of faces, their eyes half-closed and their mouths moving up and down with speech. What they said was muffled, though, because their tongues convoluted into the floor–or ceiling, whichever it was–that composed the land of tongues.

The belts that had caught me fixed my face in line with the others and dragged my tongue to its new place. I squinted from strain and asked what this was all about. My words were muffled. The only response I received was din. I kept asking.

Come and be a part of it!

Come and be a part of it! A new initiative from your Government! Do you want social justice! Do you want a good and fair world! Then be a part of our ground-breaking new program! Dr. Rapture Sviercovich of the Center for Attractive Social Justice has shown that our sexual attractions are synaptic connections formed by culture! We learn to find things sexually attractive! It's nurture! Not nature! In our new program we reset your synapses to be attracted to social justice! Thoughts of breasts, penises, clitorises, all manner of nipples, shoulders, biceps, rear ends, hips, and emotional security will be replaced by thoughts of giving to charity! Saving babies dying from diarrhea in Lesotho! Volunteering at the local homeless shelter! Tutoring dyslexic Navajo children on reservations! Come to our state-of-the-art Social Justice Resetting Facility in beautiful Speonk, Long Island! We will pay you to put wires in your brain and masturbate to images of Indonesian teenagers with goiters! Mongolian grandfathers with elephantiasis! No more pornography! No more mechanical dildos! No more failed relationships! You'll orgasm at a better world! Isn't that what you want!

Capitalism

Ahmed paints a painting: a close-up of JFK's face, pained, as he sucks a faceless woman's black breast. The title: Capitalism.

Bob and Steve Coming Together

"Are we doing it today?"
"Yes."
"Really?"
"Absolutely."
"I mean really really?"
"Didn't I tell you we would?"

Bob had promised Steve that they would try it.
Everyone was doing it. It was the hip thing for
the gay living dead.

"Really?"
"Yes."
"Okay."

Bob took his bleeding, leprous hand and
wrenched it from his wrist. His veins dangled
down like pieces of twine. Then Steve tore his
own hand from his arm. Facing each other, Bob
took Steve's wrist and gently screwed his own
hand into the place where his lover's once was.
Steve did the same. The couple stood together
in a pool of their mixed blood, gazing into each
others eyes.

"This is incredible," Steve said.

They proceeded to take each other apart, piece by piece, until they were a pile of pussing limbs on the floor of their studio loft. Then they put themselves together, mixing and matching their limbs and torsos.

"Yes," Steve moaned.

Bob took his arm and attached to one of Steve's arm sockets.

"Yes, c'mon."

Then Steve put one of his feet on one of Bob's ankles, fastening it.

"Oh God, yes..."

Bob took his right thigh and inserted it into Steve's hips.

"Yes, fuck, oh..."

Then Bob and Steve rose to their knees, holding each others arms. They shared a final embrace, putting themselves together until they were made of each other.

"Oh do it, oh, do it, yes."

Standing up, they were pieces of each other. They screamed.

"I'm coming!"

Very Short Stories Based on GRE Words[2]

---

[2] Stories > 2,000 words inspired by the meaning of words the author studied for the Graduate Research Examination.

Variegated
Many colored (adj.)

Have you ever meditated on the top of a very tall
mountain and a toucan shat on your shoulder
and you said "oh shit, a toucan just shat on my
shoulder," and an elephant walked by and
harrumphed and you asked him about the laws
of the jungle and if there were any robe-shitting
rules, and after you asked your question you
imagined that the elephant was walking with a
baby elephant that was as small as a mouse
even though elephants are supposed to be
afraid of mice, and then you imagined that this
tiny elephant was friends with all the mice in
the jungle and that this baby mouse elephant
couldn't understand why his family got so
freaked out at the dinner circle when he told
them honestly where he was spending his spare
time, and that the baby mouse baby elephant's
best friend was a mouse named Sam and that
Sam was all sorts of interesting colors and was
known throughout the forest for being the mac-
daddy with all the lady toucans, and so you
guessed that it was probably a female toucan
shitting with delight when she saw Sam
hanging out with the baby mouse elephant,
therefore causing the disruption of your search
for enlightenment?

Tractable
Docile, Easily Managed (adj.)

Grupo the sad clown could juggle chainsaws. He could hit an apple sitting on a beautiful woman's head with a knife. He could put a smile on an unhappy child's face by pulling a never-ending handkerchief made of all the colors of the light spectrum from his painted mouth.

He was also the best employee the circus had. He never got angry. When they lost funding for the elephant riding portion of his act and repot men came and took his elephants away, he didn't protest. When they fired Mammy, his trapeze-artist fiance, because she was Muslim and the manager said that no one would come to watch a circus with a terrorist in it, Grupo didn't question his manager's decision.

Yes, Grupo was an obedient clown.

One day Stoompa, the Prussian giant, approached Grupo with a look of concern.

"Grupo," he said, "I've noticed that you haven't taken off your makeup for some time, not even after shows. This doesn't seem healthy to me."

When Stoompa said this Grupo brought his hand to his cheek. He felt the old crust of a clown's face: the downward painted smile, the large painted tear falling from his eye.

"Oh," he said, blinking, "I guess I didn't even notice."

Solicitous
Nervous, Concerned (adj.)

Sylvia and Roberta sit on a set of stairs by the front door of their house. Sylvia is wearing a flower print dress and a white cardigan wrapped carefully around her shoulders. Roberta is wearing pajamas. They both lean forward with their elbows on their knees looking straight ahead. Roberta breaks a thick silence.

Do you know when he's getting here?
No.
Why not?
I told you.
No you didn't.
Yes I did.
No. You didn't.
He didn't say.
He didn't say?
He said between five and seven.
What is he, a cable guy?
I don't know.
You don't know?
I don't know.
What do you know?
I know that I met him online, that he said he was dependable, fashionable, and conventionally handsome.

Conventionally handsome?
Yes.
Okay, well...
And that he'd pick me up between five and
seven.
Are you nervous?
No.
Really?
Absolutely not.
Not even a little bit?
I'm not the slightest bit nervous. Not even a
dollop, a pinch, of nervous.
Well I'd be nervous. I'd be nervous if someone I
never met was coming to pick me up for a date
and I got all dressed up and I didn't know when
exactly he was coming and I was just standing
by the door waiting--
I guess you and I are different people, then.

The door bell rings. The two women rush to
answer it. They open the door and see a UPS
delivery man standing next to a mannequin.
The mannequin is wearing a suit. The delivery
man asks them a question.

Can one of you sign for this?

Refractory

The story we usually hear about Sir Isaac
Newton is that one day, by chance, an apple fell
and hit him on the head and inspired the theory
of gravity.

But it wasn't chance that caused the apple to
fall.
On that fine sunny day, he was leaning against
the trunk of a tree playing with a glass prism.
Newton caught a ray of sunlight in the prism
and, just as the spectrum of colors spread out
before him, a genie wearing a tweed jacket and
a powdered wig arose out of the light.

"Hello!" it declared, "I am the Occidental genie!"
Newton was horrified. The possibility of a genie
contained within the properties of light was
inexplicable to his scientific mind. But Newton,
assuring himself that there is a natural
explanation for any observable phenomenon,
regained his composure.

"Okay," he said, remembering something, "isn't
the man that frees a genie entitled to wishes?"

"Wishes?" asked the Occidental genie.

"Yes."

"For you?"

"Yes, for me."
The Occidental genie waited, rubbed his transparent chin, and said,

"Absolutely not."

"Why?" demanded Newton.

"Because I'm not that type of genie."

"Then what type of genie are you?"

"One that is nobody's slave! I do indeed have wishes to give but I've come to the conclusion that it's inappropriate to just give people what they want whenever they ask for it. I like guessing what they want and then giving it to them."

"Can't you make an exception?" Newton asked.

"Absolutely not," said the genie.

Newton paused, considering the situation.

"So what do I want?" he asked.

The Occidental genie floated close to Newton's face and said, smiling,

"You want very badly to be hit in the head."

"I can honestly say I don't want that," Newton responded.

"Yes you do," the genie insisted.

"No I don't."

"Oh yes you do, believe me."

"Not a genie at all, really," Newton said Britishly, under his breath.

"Yes I am," the genie said.

Newton became annoyed.

"No, you're certainly not," he said.

"Oh yes, I am," the genie persisted.

"No!"

"Yes."

"What kind of genie tells a man that he wants to be hit in the head?"

"One that's nobody's slave!" the Occidental genie chanted like an ancient song.

And with this the genie vanished upward into the center of the sun, becoming one with the rays of pure light streaming through the branches of the apple tree.
Frustrated with this encounter, Newton leaned back heavily against the trunk of the tree. When

he did this, his back hit the trunk with just enough force to cause a ripe apple to fall from its branch and hit him on the head.

Puerility
the state or quality of being a child. (n)

Scene: A thirteen year-old boy talks to a therapist. He squirms on a large couch, looking around. She clicks a pen, looks up at him, and asks the first question.

--So, why are you here?
--Why am I here?
--Yes. I ask every patient that.
--Oh.
--So?
--I'm here because...no, you'll think I'm stupid.
--No I won't.
--Yes you will.
--No I won't. It's my job not to think you're stupid.
--Oh.
--So. Why are you here?
--Okay. I kind of have this, like, superpower.
--Superpower?
--Yeah, superpower.
--And what's your superpower?
--It's sort of hard to explain.
--Try.
--Okay. Like, when I see people sometimes I can, like, see them at different ages.
--What do you mean by "different ages"?

--See!

--What?

--You think I'm stupid.

--No, I don't. I just want to know. It's my job to want to know.

--Oh.

--So, what do you mean by "different ages"?

--So...I mean, like, I can see you right now when you were a little kid. Like what you looked like when you were little.

--Really?

--Yeah. And sometimes I can see people when they're really old, too. Like what they'll look when they're really old.

--That's very interesting.

--Interesting?

--Yes, interesting. And so you're here because of this superpower?

--Kind of. I'm here because I had this meeting with my teacher and my parents and the principal. They all said I had to come.

--What, something happened at school?

--Well. I don't know, I guess, like, my history teacher, Ms. Brin, she was teaching and she's like, really old, like eighty-something, but I saw her when she was really young and she looked beautiful. I guess I was looking at her weird and she made me stand up in front of the class and I was, you know...

--Aroused?

--Yeah.

--Hmm.

--So we had to have this meeting because everyone thinks it's really weird for me to think that an eighty-something old woman is beautiful. They think it's inappropriate. But it's really just because of my superpower.

--Do you think that it's inappropriate to be attracted to Ms. Brin?

--I don't know. I mean, yes, like... it's weird. Of course it's weird. And inappropriate to like, go on a date with her. But I'm not gonna go on a date with Ms. Brin. It's just what I see. But people don't see it so they don't understand. Like sometimes I laugh at my parents because I see them as babies. They don't like that too much.

--I could understand that. Parents need to feel like parents. All adults need to feel like adults.

--You're right about that.

--So, how do you feel about your superpower?

--I don't think any adult ever asked me that.

--It's my job to ask you that.

--Oh.

--So, how do you feel about it?

--Well, I think its okay. I mean, it makes me confused and angry sometimes because people don't understand. But it's cool. Like this one time I was babysitting my little brother, Alex. He's six. My mom and dad were working all the time so I had to look after him. Alex and I were on the couch watching the "Muppet Babies" on TV and my mom came home all pissed off from work. I know not to say anything to adults when they're like that, all stressed out, but Alex was really happy to see her. So when she came in he said "Hi mommy!" But my mom just kept walking without saying anything back and went into the kitchen. She didn't even look at him. After that Alex was quiet for like ten minutes, looking really sad. We watched the Muppet

Babies for awhile and I looked at him, being all sad, and I saw him as a really old man, like really old. Then I looked at my mom. She was sitting at the kitchen counter drinking something and staring out the window. I saw her as a baby, like I do sometimes. She had her hand in her mouth and she was making all these baby noises. I laughed and I told Alex.
--What did you tell him?
--I told him that mom is a baby.
--And what did he say?
--Nothing. He smiled like he knew what I was talking about and got up from the couch and went over to my mom. He climbed up onto our kitchen counter and put his face really close to hers and said, "coochi-coochi-coo!!" It was so cool.
--Why did you think it was cool?
--Because to me it looked like a really old man was standing on a kitchen counter talking to a baby. And it totally was.

Proscribe
ostracize, banish (v.)

guilt   O.E. gylt "crime, sin, fault, fine," of
unknown origin, though some suspect a
connection to O.E. gieldan "to pay for, debt,"
but O.E.D. editors find this "inadmissible
phonologically."

As is evident from the etymology above, there is
confusion about the history of guilt. We will
resolve this confusion presently in the form of a
narrative. Our story begins with ostriches and
ends with a boy buried in the dirt.

No religion or theory of science mentions it, but
there was a time when ostriches were the
dominant species on earth. They had a
complete society with governments, economies,
and cultures. Their populations were densest in
what was to become Western Europe.

For our purposes, one custom ubiquitous
throughout ostrich society must be described in
detail: their system of justice. Crimes occurred
in the cities of ostriches but, given the goodness
of the animals, an ostrich crime was more
indicative of forgetfulness or absent-

mindedness than maliciousness toward other ostriches. As soon as an ostrich committed a crime, he almost always remembered the rule that had slipped his mind. Once cognizant of his mistake he went to the outskirts of the city, into the forests and fields and meadows, and found an earthy spot to bury his head in the ground until he felt confident that he would remember the rule in the future.

Therefore, ostrich society did not need a justice system per se. Criminals punished themselves.

For our purposes, it should also be noted that ostriches co-existed peacefully with other, lesser animals. Wild herds of Homo erectus, for example, roamed the undeveloped countryside, hunting and sleeping in caves.

In one such cave, near the outskirts of the ostrich capitol, a pair of Homo erectus parents gave birth to a strangely hairless and upright boy with a large head. This individual was the first Homo sapiens, though his parents could not know this. They cared for him and raised him, despite his abnormalities, feeding him nuts and berries and small mammals. Things were relatively normal until the strange boy reached adolescence. Then the problems began. When he turned sixteen, the boy began to act very oddly. He pointed at things and made strange noises that his parents didn't understand. He pointed at the ostrich cities, he pointed at the mountains, he pointed at the sun, he pointed at the valleys, and he pointed at their fire and at the walls of their cave. For each of these things he had a different noise, which he would repeat over and over again. When he made these noises, his parents merely shrugged and smiled and continued with their business, patting him on the head.

We suppose here that these noises were the first instances of human language.

One day, a particularly important day for our purposes, while hunting and gathering, the son witnessed the violent murder of a chimpanzee by a rival group of other chimpanzees. The boy attempted to resuscitate the dead chimp, but failed. He returned to his parents' cave carrying the mauled body. The chimp's face was mutilated and its arms were twisted and covered in dried blood. The son held the corpse in front of his parents, shaking it back and forth and yelling many noises, noises they'd never heard before. (This, we submit, was the first human complaint against injustice.) His mother became concerned. She reached out to her son, whose eyes were bloodshot and spilling tears, but the son, in a rage, threw the carcass of the mauled primate at his mother. Then he grabbed her arm in anger and she winced, her eyes filled with horror at her child's behavior.

His father, confused and afraid, threw himself at his son and yelled to protect his wife. The son didn't stop. He continued hurting his mother. His father grabbed the boy by the neck and dragged him to the entrance of their cave and threw him to the ground. The father blinked and pointed his hairy finger to the fields, away from their cave, toward the ostrich cities.

The son rose to his feet and ran in the direction his father pointed. Both father's and son's faces were wet with tears.

After several days of delirious wandering, the boy found the top of a small hill and looked down into the ostrich capitol. With nowhere else to go, he walked towards it.

On his way to the city he saw something he'd never seen before. In a field, spread far apart from one another, three ostriches sat with their heads buried in the ground. He stopped to consider these creatures and muttered several noises to himself. He walked on without disturbing them.

When the boy (who we must remember was the first Homo sapiens) reached the edge of the city, he was exhausted. He sat against the side of a building. Within a few minutes a delegation of ostriches quickly circled around him. The birds, communicating through complex blinks and twists of their necks, decided he was not a threat. They brought him to the hut of an ostrich that had a spare room. They gave the boy water to drink and grain to eat. They showed him a mattress of straw where he could spend the night. The boy felt safe and happy in the company of the ostriches. After eating and making many noises at the ostriches, he lay down on the straw mattress and fell into a deep sleep. The group of ostriches looked at one another, blinking in approval, and left the boy in peace.

That night there came a piercing shriek from the house where the boy slept. It was not mammalian, but avian. The scream echoed through the streets of the city and a herd of ostriches ran towards the house. Inside they found the boy beating his host with his fists, his face tensed in anger. Blood was spilled upon the dirt floor like a carpet beneath the corpse of the host ostrich.

Two of the ostriches ran to the boy and pushed him back with their necks and legs. He struggled, but was overwhelmed by the chaotic flapping and kicking all around him. Through the legs of the ostriches he saw the body of the ostrich that had been so kind to him. The boy felt a surge of confusion and pain. He began to make noises that were pitiful and sad. He cried, choking on these pieces of a language no one could understand.

After the ostriches detained him to their satisfaction, they decided what would be done with the ranting boy.
One of the stronger birds kicked him in the head and the boy passed out. Then the ostrich herd dragged him to the outskirts of their city. They dragged him over rocks and tree roots until, after much searching in the darkness, they found a flat patch of earthy ground. It was there that they buried the boy's head in the dirt, in accordance with their system of justice.

They left him. After several minutes the boy woke up, unable to breathe. His eyes, ears, nose, and mouth were filled with soil. He experienced total blackness and in this blackness he saw the body of the ostrich he had beaten to death, the face of the mauled primate, and his mother's face the night he was sent away from his home. He felt a new feeling then. It was a dull heaviness that weighed like a stone on his heart. The son lifted his head out of the ground. Dirt filled his throat and he coughed it up. As he coughed, he looked out into the night and found that he was alone. He began to cry and make a new noise, a noise he had never heard himself make before, a new word in his language that would become ours.

It sounded like "gylt, gylt."

Paucity

Earlier that evening Mr. and Mrs. Michaels sat
at opposite ends of a bar with their backs to
each other. Mr. Michaels was having drinks
with a woman that was not Mrs. Michaels, and
Mrs. Michaels was having drinks with a man
that was not Mr. Michaels. It just so happened
that they both got up to go to the bathroom at
the same time. They saw each other. Both of
them shocked, they turned around and paid
their respective bills and left together, each
driving their own car back home.

Now Mr. and Mrs. Michaels are sitting on their
living room couch staring at the wall above their
television, which is turned off.

Mr. Michaels attempts communication.

"I'm going to go get some chips from the kitchen.
Do you want any?"

Mrs. Michaels is silent.

Mr. Michaels leaves the room and comes back
empty-handed and sits down, resting his hands

on his knees.

"What do we do?"

Mrs. Michaels says nothing. Mr. Michaels tries to be specific.

"Do we talk about it?"

"I don't know if there's very much to say."

"Who was he?" he asks.

"Who was she?" she retorts.

They both lean back on the couch and look forward again at the blank television screen.

"How long?" he asks.

"Two years," she says, "you?"

"Three," he says.

Then there is silence, long, definitive, muscular. It extends several minutes. Mr. and Mrs. Michaels sigh intermittently, trying not to see each other.

"Weren't you going to go get chips?" Mrs. Michaels asks in a whisper.

"There wasn't any left," Mr. Michaels says, "so I gave up on the idea."

Mollify
Soothe (v.)

Molly's the best masseuse in Miami. Trained by
Hindu gurus in ancient anatomies, she gives
massages according to a pantheon of deific
connections. She was once a medical student at
Harvard but abandoned the pursuit of Western
medicine, noting upon her departure that it is
competitive, mechanical, and blind. Instead she
went to Juwalalumpur, India and enlisted as a
monk in a Hindu monastery whose traditions
and healing practices are said to have
originated before recorded history.
After years of study and practice, Molly now
works at the Mandarin Oriental, the most
expensive and respected resort in a land of
resorts. She smoothes the kinked backs of
businessmen and heads of state—all those
whose worldly burdens tighten and fold into the
muscles of their necks and backs.

Today we find Molly confronting her most
disturbing and difficult case: Matthew Gordian.
He has entered her parlor and she's shocked.
His body doesn't look human. He is folded in
half. His spine is bent so his hips go up and to
the left, meeting his shoulders and forming a
terrifying straight line. His legs are atrophied

around each other so the crook of one leg is wrapped around his neck, forcing his chin to fit near the end of his hipbone. His other leg is somehow stuck straight up like a periscope, its toes facing forward. These toes wiggle every minute, like a kind of facial tic. His arms are bent across what's left of his chest so his right hand is on the left side of his body and his left hand is on the right side of his body. The fingers of his right hand snap in a strange rhythm with the wiggling toes of his periscope foot.

More frightening than Gordian's body is his face, which is almost fully covered by his convoluted muscles. Only his nose and one hazel eye show through a small window made by a thigh and a wrist. This eye blinks and the nose takes in deep, silent breaths, exhaling its air forcefully with a hissing noise.

Gordian has two interns that wheel him around in a wheelchair that looks like a small hammock with bicycle wheels. Wires run from a basket on the bottom of the rolling hammock into the folded person it cradles. A small laptop computer rests in a basket at one end of the chair, the lights from the PC blinking from constant activity. There's a blackberry duct-taped to the top of the laptop and an iPod duct-taped next to it. Gordian speaks through this computer, and his words are projected from a speaker near the periscope foot.

There with his interns his one eye stares at Molly.

"Hello," he says through the speaker.

Before Gordian arrived Molly researched him, as she does with all her high-profile clients. She comes to know their lives so she can better untangle them. Gordian's dossier, an excerpt from Wired magazine, has been pinned to the wall above her desk in the massage parlor for weeks like a challenge:

"The greatest living guru of convergence culture, Matthew Gordian has funded, researched, and developed unthinkably new horizons of technological media. He has made more connections between new technologies, entertainment, and marketing than any other: blogs on TV, TV on cell phones, radios on blackberries, movies on iPods, iPods in movies, cars that parallel park for you, cars that you can talk to, cars whose speakers are connected to your iPod, cell phone, and radio. Advertising. Internet. Communication. Information. Gordian is the techno-business genius of our time."

When she first read the dossier, it sounded like familiar gibberish. She wasn't especially nervous about Gordian. He seemed like the usual mogul. But now that she sees him she can't help but think he's the strangest, most gruesome, and helpless creature she has ever seen. She isn't sure she can help him.
The interns lift Gordian onto Molly's massage table. When they put him down he shifts his tangled limbs, positioning himself, and props

his body upright with his left hand like a living ball of twine.

Molly takes a long, cleansing breath. She repeats an Upanishadic mantra and tries to accept this man and all his confusion. When she sees that he's merely flesh like any other, she regains her confidence. Molly's eyes are those of an old master, her experience that of an ascetic. They roam the lines of Gordian's unfortunate body. They search the paths of his legs and arms and spine. They trace the origins of underlying tendons and muscles. They find order in the seemingly impossible arrangement of his bones.
Her ancient mind, so knowledgeable in the human physique, takes Gordian apart and reconstructs him. After that it's only a matter of time before her fingers can do the work of soothing him back to the humanity he has so inadvertently abandoned.

As a test she runs the ends of her fingers along what she believes to be his left leg.

"What are you doing?" his electronic voice asks.

"I'm trying to figure out what to do with you," she says.

"What do you mean?"

"Well," Molly looks at the single eye, "you're a little complicated."

Gordian's toes wiggle at the top of his periscope foot.

"I know. I do not know how this happened."

"You don't?"

"One thing led to another, I suppose."

"Just try to relax."

"I have heard that before."

Molly chuckles, detecting humor in the computer's digitized tone.

"Do your best."

Molly starts with his arms. She pulls them down and turns them around one another. Bones pop, cracking from neglect. She untwists, unravels, unkinks the knotted tendons and tissues. Then she rolls Gordian's spine straight very slowly, bringing his lower half down so it lies flat on her table. With this movement she reveals the rest of his face. His mouth is blue and small and wrinkled from lack of air. His lips are pursed around a plastic tube. His cheeks and face and forehead are wet with sweat and purple from constant pressure.

Gordian's other eye, strangely blackened, blinks in this new light.

She finally stretches Gordian so he is flat on his back. His arms and legs remain slightly mangled, bent at odd angles against his frame, but his body now resembles that of a human being. His head is at the top of him and his feet are at the bottom of him. His wires fall to the ground. She takes another breath and begins an ancient Vedic massage, kneading and smoothing muscles. This takes hours but she does it with such care and concentration that she seems in a trance, meditating as she gives new life to the flesh.

When she finishes, Gordian turns his head to Molly. He's crying. Tears stain the patterned Hindu cloth draped over her table.

"Thank you," he says in his own voice.

Disinter
To take from the grave, exhume (v)

One time I was in the car with my friends and we were all in high school so they weren't really my friends and they started talking about this time when they stole a goat from Old Man Rumdle's farm out by the elementary school

and brought the goat to the cemetery nearby
and dug up this dorky kid Eugene's
grandmother that'd recently died and strapped
Eugene's dead grandmother's body to the goat
they stole from Rumdle's farm and set the goat
loose and chased it around the cemetery and
then they said that the next day at school they
told Eugene all about it and that Eugene said,

"Oh my gosh, you guys are so dead."

Selected Facestories[3]

Instead of buying things Lou takes digital pics and prints them out and places them in the places where the things would go: pics of knives in the knife holder, pics of cups in cupboard, pics of garbage in the garbage can. Lying on the pic of her bed Lou pales and flattens, starving, and takes her own digital pic to print and put in her place.

Uhoh went to war. Got captured by the enemy and woke up in a chair getting tortured, Uhoh. The man doing it was his long lost brother, Haha. I know you! You're my brother! Uhoh pleaded, Let me go! We'll go see our mother together! Shot Uhoh in the chest, Haha. Watching the spy die he saw his own face on the corpse, Haha. Lost in blood, Uhoh.

My love looks at me and my heart breaks out of
my chest. It jumps on the table and salsa
dances with our salsa, mash-potatoes with our
mashed potatoes, and cuts a rug with our
butter knife. Joy is ours. Then my heart gets
greedy: opens its veiny mouth, eats my love,
and leaves us both for dead in the diner,
dancing its eating dance out the door.

Ta's mother was human trafficked to Dubai and he learned the world. Ta's brother worked an iPhone factory and killed himself and he learned the world. Ta's father was stabbed in a drunken knife fight and he learned the world. Ta's sister died from toxic drinking water and he learned the world. Ta starved himself to death in a cage outside the President's house and he taught the world.

Adam Smith walked his pet polar bear Hand through the arctic. Wearing matching speedos they discussed the northern lights. Colorful, said Smith. Magical, said Hand. The pair growled with pleasure. They came upon a community penguins, pooping white poop and mating. Hand ate one and disappeared. Smith, distraught, exclaimed: Hand, you're invisible! Then he damned all penguins and wrought the market as revenge.

I befriended a graffiti artist named I. We went to brunch. I ordered an omelet and I got huevos rancheros. We ate and talked, I and I. I hate the conformists, I said. I know! I replied. They don't stop copying my graffiti designs, I complained. It's such a shame, I commiserated. Just be yourself—paint what you paint, be what you are, I recommended. I sighed: If only it were that simple.

The cafe plays indie rock. The kitchen, bachata.
For Juan outside=English, inside=Spanish.
Today a woman at her laptop. Beautiful, skinny
jeans, pale skin. Juan leaves the kitchen to talk
to her. In the hall near the bathrooms, a
passage between where musics mix, Jose, line
chef, asks, Que haces loco? Juan waits in the
noise between worlds. The woman leaves. Hasta
la proxima, corazon, he says returning to his
music.

Short Stories[4]

The Answer is Gail

Dr. Nathan, called 'Doc' by his Filipino nurse, looks down at the white carpet of his office. His hand waves above the filing cabinet drawer like it's lost, his blue blind eyes darting back and forth.

"I can't write letters that way anymore. They're poignant, precise, meaningful. She brought that out in me. Did I... were you the one that took down a letter last time?" he asks.

"I don't think so," I say.

"Well, I was writing a letter and when I was done I had to ask whoever it was if it was good. I don't think I'll ever get used to that."

Dr. Nathan is ninety-five years old. He is a blind professor Emeritus of English literature. He pays me eleven dollars an hour to come to his home in suburban Virginia and read poetry, stories, the day's mail, encyclopedia entries, and etymologies to him.

I cradle a manila folder he's asked me to excavate from his files. The name "Gail" is written on it in black sharpie. It contains a few faded letters dating back to the 70's. They're from a correspondence he had with a student a few years after she graduated. She had made the first move: a nervous attempt to get in touch with a memorable mentor. I read it aloud to him. It seems like she realized too late how important he was to her. She needed him. She wanted him to read her poetry.

I can picture her. She's a young woman five years out of undergraduate: bouncing brown hair curled up at the end, small chin, a smiling oval face. Her teeth are idiosyncratic, small and darkened from cigarettes; straight. She probably sat at her old college desk scribbling in a fury fueled by some precarious whim. Maybe she was trying to locate a lost part of herself, purring as words geysered from her. Maybe she had literary fantasies. But maybe she needed confirmation. Some qualified objective opinion. Someone to tell her that fame was waiting for her. She needed someone of poetic repute, someone who knew what they were talking about when they called her a genius. So, one humid night, instead of stanzas came paragraphs. And in the title's place was: 'Dear Prof Nathan.'
Nathan closes his clouded eyes as I speak her words. Type-written black ink on tattered paper. Her sentences are sharp and direct, but nothing is capitalized. The caps button on her typewriter must have been broken.

"What do you think of her as a correspondent?" he asks me.

"She seems like an interesting character."

"Yes. I enjoyed reading her letters because she
was honest, no 'how are you feeling' or 'how is
the weather.' She was straight forward, said
what she felt. She communicated. She seemed
always to have something to offer."

He asks me to read another. I do.

What he calls honesty is more of an emotional
purity. Nathan calls her honest because she
never edited herself fearing his opinion.
She seemed to write herself into these letters
without apprehension or censor, as if that
aspect of drunkenness had spilled into
her writing style during college. Her words make
him giggle, his face wrinkling like an old man's
face might when remembering younger days.
Maybe he's remembering the feeling of an
inexperienced heartbeat; the way it thumps in a
great big world of things to learn.

"It's odd," he chuckles, "she thought I was being
chauvinistic in a story I sent her and I
disagreed with her in a somewhat harsh way.
 We stopped writing to each other after that. I
think she felt insulted."

His ancient lips part, smiling.

"I was teaching in Connecticut some years later
and I left to attend a conference in Utica. She
was doing social work there at the time. I wrote
to her saying that I'd be in town. At Rome, a few

stops from Utica, a woman walked on the bus and I thought it looked exactly like her."

"Did you say something?" I ask.

"No, I'm timid in some ways. I just looked at her and she looked back at me, but her expression didn't change."

He puts a hand to his chin and closes his eyes. "She sat in front of me that whole bus ride. I realize I could have said 'Gail' in between the seats, and if she didn't want to take notice then she could have ignored me. I really could have..." he trails off for a second—he whimpers a little.

"So did you meet her once you got to Utica?" I break the quick silence.

"No," snapping out of it, "she didn't write me back before I left and I didn't get in touch with her when I arrived. A few weeks after that conference I moved permanently to Florida. I haven't heard from her since those letters."

A dusty pause passes and Nathan looks down at his lap. After a few seconds he looks up in my general direction and seems surprised. At times like these, I think he falls asleep for several seconds. When he wakes up he usually asks me one question from consistent group of three or four that have no relation to what we're doing. He either asks about the origin of my name, what I'm studying, or what I'm going to do with my life, his voice crackling like an old fire.

"Did you say you wanted to be a professor?"

"I've said that, yeah."

"Tough to get a job, but I think it's worth it."

"I know," I smile. He asks me what we were doing.

"I was reading from your letters to Gail."

"Oh yes. Are there any more letters there?"

"No, I think we've gone through them all," I say.

"Alright, then, put the file back."

Dust plumes up from the folder with his 1945 tax receipts and I stuff Gail's file exactly where I found it: way in the back.

My two roommates, a friend from Boston and his girlfriend Lauren, want to see a movie I've already seen. I walk with them to the theater to get some air. The three of us stroll along the riverside where large groups of twenty-somethings nurse expensive drinks at an outdoor bar. Their ties are undone or loosened. It's happy hour. They move back and forth. They sit down and standing up. They grab each others arms in the wake of empty jokes about their bosses and co-workers.

Four women walk by ready to enter the bar.
Clad in high heels, they look like four front
halves of horses: calf muscles on display
and clip-clopping in line. Lauren looks at them.

"You see them? That'll be us soon," she says.

"Very soon," Eric replies.

Outside the bar, I see a younger woman sitting
on a bench. I look at her long enough to see her
shoes and what she's doing. She's wearing old
sandals. She's jotting things down in a
notebook. The sandals look handmade. We keep
walking.

When we get to the movie theater. Eric and
Lauren buy their tickets and I decide not to see
the movie. I tell them I'll meet them in a few
hours.

"What are you going to do?" Eric asks.

"I don't know, I'll probably just take a walk and
read somewhere or something."

I head back towards the river. The sun is
setting. I see a tour boat leaving in a few
minutes and I ambivalently inquire about the
price.

Browsing the benches beside the water, I pick
an open spot. I throw my weight down, cross my
right leg over my left, and dig out my book. The
woman sitting next to me is jotting things down

in a notebook. I look at her toes beneath the hem of a tan skirt. Handmade sandals. I look up from my book and over at her.
Her brown hair rests shining on her shoulders in the twilight.

I stare at the book. I can't read the words. My eyes bounce up and down the page. I glance over at her. I realize that I can say something or not say anything, wonder or not wonder, have someone new to remember or stay timid.

"Excuse me, why do you like writing on graph paper?"

Turning her face towards me, she rests her small chin on her shoulder. She smiles.

Our discussion moves from notebooks to pens, and if they'll become obsolete. We hope it never comes to that.

"When you type on a computer," she says, "you can't tell it's you. Like, if I typed this and you typed something and we put them next to each other, there'd be no way to tell who wrote it. Could have been anybody," she theorizes.

"Interesting."

The conversation jumps around excitedly and lands the ever present topic of where our lives are going. She's in graduate school getting her doctorate in English. Right now she's on vacation, just relaxing. I tell her I've been looking for a job, and found the one with Dr. Nathan.

"Oh, what's his name? I feel like one of my friends said she was working for a blind English professor."

"Norman Nathan?"

She pauses and looks up, resting her hand on her small chin.

"No, I don't know, that doesn't sound familiar."

"Oh, well." I release some air.

I reveal to her that I'm still in undergraduate and she says, "Enjoy it."

We discuss academics a bit more and I tell her I want to teach.

"You know, everyone's being encouraged not to go into academics right now because the market is flooded. Too many Ph.D's. In a few years there'll probably be more jobs."

"Yeah? I haven't heard that one yet. Sounds reassuring."

"Makes sense right?" she pauses and looks me straight in the eyes, "I say go to grad school. Have fun. It's worth it."

She means it, too. I believe everything she says.

We keep talking for a few more minutes and there's a lull in the conversation. She closes her eyes slowly, opens them again, and nods her head to signify the end. She gathers her things to leave.

"It was nice meeting you," she says. "You should try the graph paper, honestly."

"Alright. I'll try it."

Just as her eyes leave mine I feel the rumble of a question in my throat. I stop myself from asking it. I already know the answer.

The answer is Gail.

Something in the Ones and Zeros

It's definitely possible to be a cynical believer in clairvoyant dreamers. What I mean is that it's reasonable to believe that this world is capable of producing someone who can go to sleep, have a dream, and be reasonably confident that the events of that dream will occur in the near future.

My roommate Robert says that we all have the right to realize our dreams. But I don't think that's what I'm talking about. Plus, Robert doesn't really exist so I don't have to take what he says seriously.

What I mean is this: we dream at night. No one doesn't dream. Sometimes people say they don't dream, but they really do. (I learned this in a psychology class.) They just wake up feeling like they didn't dream. But I wake up feeling like I dreamed every morning. Like this morning, Sunday, I remembered the dream I dreamed where my roommate Robert went to Argentina to visit his girlfriend who worked with bees there and they decided to travel all over and see the countryside in a rented car, but they blew a flat tire while they were driving, in my dream, and they spent days walking around trying to find someone. But they couldn't find anybody and they laid down in the middle of the road together and yelled until they couldn't anymore and died.

At least they were together. That's what I thought when I woke up.

Now you could say that Robert won't actually die on a road trip with a girlfriend who works with bees in Argentina. You could say that I just dreamed it up. You'd have a good case for this. Robert's girlfriend works in Bolivia, not Argentina. She doesn't work with bees, either. Actually, one of Robert's ex-girlfriends works with bees. In Tunisia. And Robert's girlfriend actually works at a nursing station. She helps people who get a particular kind of parasite from dirty water that grows underneath their skin and forms a big boil and a fully grown worm bursts out of the boil and crawls away.

Robert's actually an international type of guy. He wouldn't get caught dead without a spare tire on a road trip. He reads the New York Times every Sunday front to back. Every single section. He also reads the Economist front to back. And when he reads, he looks up all the words he doesn't know and writes them down in a notebook. When he finds a word he doesn't know, he usually waits a day or so until he can remember what it means. Then he asks me if I've ever heard of the word and I say "no" and he tells me what it means. He runs three miles on Sundays, too. Even when it snows. And when he comes back from running his three miles he does 100 push ups right in front of me on the living room floor and audibly counts each one. Sometimes Robert does push ups even if he hasn't run three miles. He just does them to be healthy. He also swims every day at a community pool a few blocks away from our apartment. Robert's also a vegetarian and does his own taxes in February to get the biggest return possible.

But, like I said, Robert doesn't exist. Gale my therapist says so. She says he's just a symptom of my depression and anxiety. She says I fabricate Robert's good and admirable habits and accomplishments because mine aren't as good. She says that I have a complex and she assures me that the whole thing is purely chemical. This is why every time I go to see Gale, which is three times a week, she insists that I take mood-enhancing drugs to help me with my chemical disease. But I always say no because I fear the post-industrial mechanization of the human soul, which is something that I saw on the cover of a new release at Blockbuster Video. When I tell her this she shrugs and says that if I believe that, then I'll have to keep living with Robert.

Anyway, get this: Robert told me a few days ago about two friends of his that were actually traveling in Argentina together and blew a flat tire and died because they couldn't find anyone to help them. And Robert is actually going to visit his girlfriend in Bolivia this week. This is interesting because it sort of fits with my dream.

It's Monday morning and Robert and I are eating breakfast at the fold out table in our kitchen.

"I'm leaving tomorrow," he says.

"You shouldn't go, Robert," I warn him.

"Why not?"

"Because I had a dream where you died."

"Really?"

"Yeah."

"Well," he stops to think, "I think I'll take the risk."

"But you might die," I insist.

"It'd be better to go than not go, I think."

"Why?"

"Because I want to go. You have to do what to want to do. Or else life isn't worth living."

Robert does whatever he wants to do. But he always does good things. Like he volunteers for Habitat for Humanity and he reads a lot of books about morality that talk about what Goodness is and whether or not we just make it up as we go along. He also makes a lot of charitable donations, which he itemizes on his list of deductibles when he does his taxes two months in advance.

"But you might die," I repeat.

"I think that would be okay, as long I'm doing what I want to be doing when it happens."

He sits and peels a grapefruit (Robert always tries to eat healthy things) on the fold out table. He holds the grapefruit at arm's length so he doesn't get any juice on his clothes. He is wearing a pressed white shirt and a tie because he is going to work. I am wearing my robe and pajama pants and a dirty undershirt. I'm not going to work because I don't have a job. I am independently wealthy. I am independently wealthy because my grandparents started a very successful soda company that my parents continue to run very successfully. They sell soda all around the world and they want me to be happy so they pay for my rent, my food, my therapist bills and my entertainment. But I don't need much entertainment. I don't do much of anything. I talk to Robert when he has the time in between work and volunteering and reading and exercising. I go to see Gale three times a week. And I do two other things that I haven't mentioned. Whenever I have an emotion, any emotion at all, I write either a 1 or a 0 on a wall in the kitchen that I call my wall of emotions. If I have an emotion and there's a 0 at the end of the last line, then I put a 1 next to it. If I have an emotion and there's a 1 at the end of the last line, then I put a 0 next to it. I've been doing this since I moved in, which was a week after I graduated from college. The night I moved in I sort of randomly decided to write a small 0 at shoulder height on the wall in the kitchen. I guess I didn't know what else to do.

There are a lot of 1 and 0 marks on the wall of emotions. Robert asks me about it sometimes. I think he thinks I'm an artist. But I'm not trying to make the wall look like anything, which definitely means I'm not an artist.

The other thing I do is walk everyday to the Blockbuster Video store around the corner from our apartment and read the titles of the new releases that are on the new releases rack. Nobody talks to me at the Blockbuster. I don't meet anyone there. Everyone just comes and rents a movie and leaves. They have different people working there all the time, so none of them recognizes me. I walk in and walk out and it doesn't matter.

Robert finishes his grapefruit and gets up and walks away. He says "goodbye" as he closes the door and I try to say "goodbye" as soon as I can but Robert shuts it as I speak. Then I get up and I write a 1 next to a 0 on the wall of emotions.

So, like I said, it's possible to be a cynical believer in clairvoyant dreamers. Because the chemicals in our brains, the ones in the synapses, I think, keep working when we're asleep. They take all the thoughts and images you experience during the day and mix them up together and register them chemically in your memory. This is why dreams seem crazy: they're made of all your experiences, but mixed up into something totally different than what you're used to. And when they get ordered into something new like that they feel just like another experience, only weirder. But even if you think dreams are just chemicals swirling around in your head, even if you think that there are no magical clairvoyant powers and people are just brain chemicals and synapses, you can still believe that there are some people who can tell the future. Because there's a chance that some of those new orderings that the brain makes when it's asleep will be accurate depictions of the future.

For instance: I had a dream last week that I was getting married to Parker Posey, and the night before our wedding I had to pick up a white Cadillac with my bike and attach the white Cadillac to the back of my bike with a yellow strap and drag it to Parker Posey's house for the rehearsal dinner.

Then, the next day, the morning after I woke up from that dream, I saw a movie poster with Parker Posey on the front of it when I was at Blockbuster. And when I left Blockbuster I saw a pickup truck at the intersection outside the Blockbuster dragging a Honda Civic behind it with a yellow strap and there was a white Cadillac right behind it. I thought that alone was interesting, but then things got more interesting. The white Cadillac that was behind the civic ran a red light at the intersection and hit a homeless man who was wearing a wedding dress. He was pushing a big dirty cart full of cans and newspapers and blankets that went flying through the air when he got hit.

It's Thursday and Robert gets home from work and starts to pack for his trip to Bolivia. He packs some clothes, but not too many because Robert can live very sparely. He trained himself to not need very much. Then he pays his bills for the month at the table. He has loans to pay from college because he was the first one in his family to graduate from college, and his parents don't make very much money at all. Then he ties a pair of boots to his hiking bag and fills up his water bottle for the flight.

"How's the wall coming?" he asks.

"Alright. It's funny because it's starting to look like something."

"You mean a picture?"

"More like some words, I think."

Robert suddenly drops to the floor and does some push ups. He counts loudly as he does them. He gets up after he says "fifty" and faces me again.

"What does it say?" he asks, panting.

"I'm not sure."

"Hmm," he says.

Then he puts his backpack on and clips a small clip across his chest and then a bigger one across his waist and then he walks away.

"Bye," he says.

"Alright," I try to say, "see you when you get back." But he shuts the door before I can finish.

I get up and make a small 0 next to a 1 on the wall of emotions.

It's a week later now, another Thursday, and I'm very convinced that we can be cynical believers in clairvoyant dreamers because earlier this morning I got a phone call from a woman who said she was Robert's mother. She sounded upset. I asked her if she really knew Robert. She said that yes, of course she knew him and that he was her son for Christ's sake. She was sniffling into the phone and started crying. She said that Robert died in Bolivia with his girlfriend because they got food poisoning in a remote mountain town and couldn't find medical help in time.
"At least they were together," I told her, not knowing what else to say.

Since then I've been making all kinds of 1 and 0 marks on the wall of emotions because, for starters, Robert was a real, actual person the whole time he was living in my apartment. On top of that, I dreamed that he was going to die a few nights before he actually did. And, on top of it all, last night I dreamed that the 1 and 0 marks on my wall of emotions really had a sentence written in them. In my dream they said:

"Fear the post-industrial mechanization of the human soul."

Man Writing Story With Ears Plugged About Painter Who Only Hears in Color, Black Ink, 2002

Ready, here we go. It's got to be a she. Sit down.
She splatters paint everywhere, yeah
everywhere. On glass, like Pollack, like a crazy
woman. She bows down to the ground like to a
thunderstorm way off in the distance in purple
gobs and bubbles way off. The paint splatters
and she screams so the glass shakes and her
throat gives out while the splotches pour from
her mind and her brain and those evil
transmitters, but are they evil? They don't have
to be evil--it should be what you were made like,
how you came, could she do this if she weren't
like this, if the doctors weren't there and the
people weren't there shimmying around her
with no idea what they were talking about?
Could you live that way? Right, of course, her
little girl inside does and cries all night and
Mommy comes and is just as confused while
the night time stars spark out like the specks of
cheap paint on her canvas, on her glass, on her
floor.

You shouldn't be worried-- she shouldn't be
worried-- neither of you can hear.

She's on her knees and you're on the chair and
she's scraping her claws on the chalkboard and
you're sitting here typing with those evil things
in your ears. Evil? Do they have to be evil?
You're doing it for your art, your expression,
like she does. Could you live any other way? It
could be just the way you came. Do you want to
go to work and live the way everyone else does
and dream dreamless nights and see nothing
when you wake and think nothing when
linguistic sound waves travel through the air
and hit you? They hit her too, but you're trying
to block them off when she just lets them hit,
when she just lets them hit.

She splatters paint everywhere and all she can
see is her mind and those swirling eclipses of
moons and slow milky pools of water like when
an oar pushes through on a lake. Everywhere.

She's got to be beautiful, just like Audrey. She's
got this curly hair and a sexy thoughtless type
of action so guys will stop in their tracks, be
distracted from their conversations to keep their
eyes on her for just one more moment so that
maybe when you, they, go to bed at night they
can have an image, some coal black hair, some
tortured artist going to buy paint that they can
have an ugly affair with in the bathroom of the
supplies shop. "Do you like this blue?" "Yeah,
you know, I feel like I've known you for years..."
That's all it takes and you're, they're, with her
in a small room, not a real room, but like in
porn with a small wave back and forth back and

forth and back and forth with dim red lights
making your, their, skin that crazy yellow hue.

She walks into the store though, and she walks
out, she doesn't say a word because the guy at
the register knows her, knows her that well,
and she buys her brushes and bottles and
tubes and with nods completes the only
transaction besides that of the diner she goes to
for every meal. The greasy spoon where her
early work hangs, where the gallery owners first
put their hands to their mouths when getting
lunch on the way back to the city. And guy at
the diner, like the paint store guy, knows her
well enough to give her a Caesar salad and a
chocolate milkshake. Yeah, just like that diner
at home. She'll go in, nod just like she's buying
paint and he'll know, like the way you've always
wished those waitresses knew what you were
going to order before you ordered it. They don't
know you're a regular but he knows her, she
gets the same thing every time and doesn't have
to say anything. Because she can't.

You can. You do. You fill the air with waves and
you think those sounds mean so much, don't
you, so much that a void just sounds like a
hummmmm a hummm like it sounds like right
now like it sounds right now just a buzz with a
tone, a pitch. With just your voice rumbling in
your throat. The mind can't make sense of the
silence; it needs to explain it so it hears
something that's not there.

She hears it all. She knows the silence, her
mind makes sense of it. She splatters paint

everywhere, you can see it on the walls of the diner, yeah, and yeah she painted the restaurant a mural one day and they all watched. Yeah, there's a story. They all watched her do it because no one ever knew how or why she could produce such screams, such images from nothing. Artie wrote her a note, once, and what did she do? She closed her eyes, opened them right into his, right through his, and nodded yes. The next day she came with her tool box, it's a red tool box, a little rusty thing with shelves that pop out like that congressman's make up artist's box. Red and crazy all over. Yeah, she just comes in and dips a wash towel into a creamy white and throws it against the wall. She hums a muffled song like this one you're hearing right now, like this you're hearing right now. She opens her mouth for the first time and all the regulars are just dumbfounded because they know the sounds she's making: they remember when they held their ears and heard themselves speak or shout like that to try and ignore the pain, to let words and noises go by unheard and unfelt, because it's better that way, right? They her working and look at their hands like they don't know how she's doing it because there's a fork in their left and knife in their right and she's throwing dishtowels against a wall.

She dips her hand into a darker brown and swirls in fisted into the pearl and it's her milkshake waiting for her under the silver box with fifties writing behind the counter. Artie smiles, big smile. There's a crowd all around and they know who she is, they've seen her on

78

the local evening news and read little articles
here and there about her shows and seen
pictures of fancy looking sophisticates with
goatees and New York City smiles with her
under their arm. They know. But they can't
believe what they're seeing, what they're hearing;
what they're not. The deconstruction, what's
getting in her way? Nothing is getting in her way.
It's the absolute breakdown of a mind and the
composition of its reconstruction-- upon a wall
that used to have phone numbers and
FuckYous written on it.

That's just like this, just like you're doing right?
There's no one around you though. There's no
wall. It's ok, probably someday...but why? Why
do you need a circle of people around you who
know you from articles and smiles and nods?
Why?

She would still compose. She did it when she
was, when you were, nine, yeah, and when no
one was watching her, you, and she would
scream like that into the painted echoes, like
you hear now, when no one in the world could
listen in the woods. In the woods by a lake
where she, you, used to camp with your friends
from school. There's a hammock there she, you,
would crawl into and sing that choked song.

Hmm...

Yeah. Write her a note, write her a note like the
guy behind the counter did, she'll hear you.
Scratch it like she would.

Would you still do this if no one were around?
Would you still throw your mind and colored
words onto paper if no one ever saw it? Would
you?

Then, she splatters words onto the paper below
the neat script with a charcoal. She pushes it in
front of you but before you can read it she takes
your head in her hands, they're your hands,
and she stuffs her, your, fingers in your ears
and sings into your eyes. You know what that
napkin says; you know what that napkin says.
You know what she's, you're, saying.

"Yes. Yes I would."

Jon and Maeve

At the bar the lights were low and green and
everyone's faces were close together and they
were laughing and talking loud so they could
hear each other over the music and some of
them played pool and others sat at tables and
leaned forward into one another and others
played darts and everyone brought up beer
bottles or glasses to their mouths and sipped
them and the bartender took orders for drinks
and the men and women that bought the drinks
held them at the height of their stomachs and
they laughed and when there were pauses in
the conversations they would sip the drinks and
look away or laugh and sometimes they all
sipped their drinks together.

Maeve Fesnying sat with Vicki Sord who was a
reporter at the Blue Ash News and they laughed
and talked and Sord had thick blond hair that
was curly and she was thin and wore bright red
lipstick and tight purple pants and Maeve
talked and laughed and drank her drink with
Sord and their faces were close.

A few stools away a man with a beard and a
round face and auburn hair mixed with gray

and dark brown sat by himself with a mug of steaming tea in front of him and his shoulders were slumped over and down to the bar and there was an oval stain of blood on the right thigh of his khakis but no one could see this because his thighs were tucked beneath the bar and his head hung over the mug so the steam of the tea rose up into his face and he breathed the steam in and sighed it out.

Maeve laughed a loud laugh and the man with the tea and the beard looked up at her and his eyes rested on her for a moment and his eyes rested there for long enough to see that her hair was curly and her face was sharp there in the dark by the bar and that she was wearing a purple button down shirt with large orange buttons and the man with the tea sat upright and his shoulders turned back and his lower lip tucked into his teeth and he stared at Maeve for a few seconds and Vicki Sord wiped her red lipsticked mouth and excused herself to the ladies' room and Maeve watched her walk off and turned to face the bar and sip her drink and she looked to her left and noticed the man with the tea and the beard staring at her and even in the low green light of the bar she could see his eyes were very blue and she saw the roundness in his cheeks and she sipped her drink again and leaned toward him and said into the noise and the music of the place,

"Do you have a girlfriend?"

The man with the tea blinked and wagged his head and looked around and away from her eyes and her eyes were smiling and he said,

"I'm sorry, I wasn't..."

"But do you?"

"Do I what?"

"Have a girlfriend."

"No. I'm...No. I don't."

Maeve leaned in closer to him and blinked a slow blink and said,

"Well, I do. I have a girlfriend. Just to let you know."

The man shook his head and put his shoulders down again and said into his tea,

"I'm sorry."

"What?"

"I said 'I'm sorry'."

"I didn't mean to make you feel sorry. It's just a line I use on guys that stare at me in bars."

The man took a deep breath and looked into his tea again and brought his face up to Maeve and said,

"Sorry. I just couldn't help noticing your shirt."

Maeve looked down at herself and she moved closer to him and said,

"You like it?"

The man brought his hands up to the bar and they were shaking and he sipped his tea with his shaking hands and said,

"I bet I know where you bought it."

"Really?"

"Yup."

She leaned in and he could smell her breath and she said,

"Five bucks says you can't."

The man put his elbows on the bar and put his face in his hands and rubbed his face and looked back at her and said,

"It's not really new, is it?"

"To me it is."

"You bought it at a thrift store, right?"

"Nope," she said and sipped her drink.

"Yes you did."

"No I didn't."

"Yes. You bought it at a thrift store in a town in Iowa. Ottumwa, Iowa."

When he said this Maeve's eyes opened wide and her face went out to his face and she said,

"Get the hell out of town! How did you know that? I was just in Ottumwa for work last week."

"The Salvation Army, right? Next to the Target and the courthouse."

"Stop it! Yes, absolutely. Yes. How the hell did you know that?"

"Do you really want to know?"

"Yeah. Yes. I do."

The man tucked his lower lip into his teeth again and said,

"I just donated all my parents' clothes to the Salvation Army in Ottumwa. That's my mom's shirt."

"Why'd you donate their clothes?"

"They died about a week ago."

Vicki Sord was out of the bathroom now and talking to a woman by the dart board and didn't see Maeve drop her drink on the floor but she heard glass shatter and Vicki looked in the direction of the noise and she saw Maeve hug the man with the tea and hold him there at the

bar while the steam from his tea steamed up
from the mug.

Maeve hugged him and kept hugging him and
he put an arm around her and her breath was
on his ear and it was warm and she was warm
and she pressed herself into him and he let his
hand rest on her lower back and his nose
pressed into the purple shirt and it smelled like
home to him and he said,

"Thanks."

"I'm so sorry. I can't believe it," she said.

"It's okay, thank you."

"No, I'm sorry. I'm so so sorry."

The man laughed and it was first time anyone
had touched him in a long time and Maeve
released him and looked at him and lunged into
him again with a big hug and locked his arms
to his sides so he couldn't move and she said,

"I can't believe your parents died and I'm
wearing your dead mother's shirt. I'm so sorry."

"I appreciate it. Thanks."

She leaned back and looked down at herself
again and started unbuttoning the orange
buttons of the shirt and she wasn't wearing
anything underneath it and the man put his
hands out to stop her and said,

"Oh, no, please, it's fine. Keep it on..."

"No. I can't believe I'm wearing your mother's shirt and your mother's dead."

"Listen, please, I–I don't even know your name yet."

Maeve stopped and took a breath and put a hand on her forehead and she wavered around and smiled and looked at this man and said,

"Hah!"

Vicki Sord walked over to the bar and sipped her drink and said,

"What's going on over here?"

Maeve turned around and blushed and said,

"Give this man five dollars."

"What?" Sord asked.

"Give him five dollars. He deserves it. He won a bet."

"What bet?"

"It's nothing," he said.

"Nothing?" Maeve asked.

The man's face fell back to his mug of tea and he put his hands around it to warm them and his shoulders fell again toward the bar and he said,

"Don't worry about it."

Maeve looked at Vicki and Vicki's eyelids were drooping and she was smiling at everything and said,

"Do you have your little pad, Vick?"

"Yeah I do."

"And a pen?"

"Yeah, yeah hold on."

Vicki reached inside of her purse and handed Maeve a journalist's notebook and then reached in again and picked out a pen and handed the pen to Maeve and Maeve took the notebook and the pen and pushed them to the man with the beard and the tea and said,

"Write your name and where you live and I'll bring you the shirt back."

"It's really not necessary."

"No no no. Let me. I'll bring five bucks with it or something."

And the man looked at her and her hand was on her hip and her hip was out and he saw her Converse sneakers and the curve of her thigh where her hand rested and he said,

"Okay."

Then he took the notebook and the pen and he wrote his name and an address and a phone number and he slid the pad and pen back to Maeve and she ripped the paper out of the pad and folded it and put it in the pocket of her jeans and she stuck out her hand and said,

"Good. I'm Maeve by the way."

"I'm—"

"No wait!"

She took the paper out of her pocket while holding his hand in mid-shake and read it aloud,

"Nice to meet you Rubber American Jon Sowse."

"Rubber American's where I work, it's not..."

"Jon, it's a pleasure."

"Well, it's nice to meet you Ma..."

"Maeve, like May with a 'v'."

"Maeve," he said.

"Right," she said.

"So I'll see you tomorrow or something?" she asked.

"Okay."

"Good."

Then Maeve turned back to Vicki and Vicki asked,

"Did you just get his number?"

"Yeah."

"But you're gay, I thought."

"No no no no no. You got it all wrong. I'm not anything."

Then Vicki and Maeve laughed and the music was loud and Maeve drank her own drink and put the piece of paper back into her jeans and she looked back to Jon whose dead mother's shirt she was wearing but he was gone into the green light and the music.

Because We're The Impressives

We're driving down 95 south to wreck my car on purpose and I remember Robert's name for us. Not just the four of us in the car, but the people like us, our friends and their friends and the people we all meet at parties where the friends of our friends get together and laugh and drink and listen to the same music.

He calls us the Impressives.

Why does he call us that?

We were sitting together on a hillside when I came up with the idea to drive my car south to our nation's capitol and have a charity event where people could pay money per minute to hit my car with a sledgehammer. I had seen this kind of charity event before at a Presbyterian Church in our town and it amazed me to see how long the line for the event was. I asked a volunteer, a fat kind of woman selling brownies with sprinkles, and she said that the church had bought an old car from a used car salesman and that they had been doing this for years because they make four times the amount of money they spend on the car. I stood and watched for an hour while people took the sledgehammer from an old man's hand, paid him, and beat the hell out of a Dodge Caravan, an old model with the crystal in the hood piece. Teenagers, tweenagers, twentysomethings, middle-aged men and women, and even some older men sent themselves into the car, denting the doors and cracking the windows and beating the hubcaps until they flew off.

One guy who looked a little older than me seemed to lose control of himself and smashed the windshield until pieces of it were everywhere. There was a moment when the glass hadn't shattered but was cracking and cracking after every hit that the man screamed this primal kind of scream, and when he did it the glass shattered and went everywhere and people in line started clapping.

Anyway, I had found out that day, the day the four of us were sitting on the hillside, that my parents wanted to get rid of our old Nissan Pathfinder truck to get a newer one, and several days before that I'd read in the newspaper that Washington, D.C. has one of the largest homeless populations in our country, that about one in five children living in the District of Columbia don't have a house and only eat one meal a day. I thought: How unjust that in the most powerful country in the world, the capitol of that country has the most homeless people? We were sitting on a hill where my Dad's office building sits looking out over the Danbury Airport and the Danbury Fair Mall. I had my ankles crossed and little twigs were itching at the back of my legs and I groaned because it was annoying and I had to keep scratching and that and the mall and the airport and the four of us sitting there next to the old Pathfinder all made me think of the homeless children in Washington, D.C.

Why did all that make me think of them?

My father is a real estate and zoning lawyer and works on that hill overlooking the mall and the airport. Robert's father is a chemical engineer. Patrick's father is a lead salesman for a chemicals corporation in town. Maya's father is a third-term congressman that represents our congressional district. My mother is a corporate writer. Rob's mother owns her own international music business. Patrick's mother is a sales representative for a drug company in New York City. Maya's mother is a middle school teacher. Danbury is located in Fairfield County. Fairfield County is considered, at this time, to be the wealthiest county in the United States.

Why does any of this matter?

Robert, Patrick, Maya and I go to Danbury High School where we are in the honors program. Right now I'm working for Maya's father's re-election campaign, Maya is working in my father's law firm, Patrick is interning with Robert's father at his engineering firm, and Robert was going to be an assistant in Patrick's father's company but instead he started working at a nursery hauling mulch onto mulch trucks. He said he wanted to work with his body.

Why did Robert decide to haul mulch instead of intern somewhere, and why does this make me nervous?

Robert has had a rough year. He told me a couple days ago that he had a nervous breakdown while visiting colleges because he couldn't hide the fact that he wasn't eating anymore except maybe a piece of bread during the day because he felt that that was the only way to feel like he had any control over his life. Robert and I are very good friends. He's seemed weird over the past few months, but I couldn't sense anything was wrong. Actually, there wasn't a lot of time to talk between our classes and homework, and he was going away every weekend on college trips with his parents so I didn't really see him.

But he said that on the last college visit he went on, the weekend before we were all sitting on the hill, that he woke himself up screaming and that he was sweating and had clenched his nails into his fists so tightly that he was bleeding from little slits in his palms and his parents ran over to him and asked him if he was alright he looked around and he said he didn't know.

Why did he wake up screaming?

We're passing through Princeton Junction on 95 south and Maya says:

"I don't think I'll get in."

"Where?" I ask.

"Princeton."

Robert sighs.

"You'll get in," Patrick says.

"I don't know, you know? I mean, I didn't do great on my SATs and my grades aren't that great."

"You've always gotten A's!" Patrick retorts.

"I wonder if my grades are good enough," I say.

"Oh my God you're so smart, Dave," Maya says.

Robert exhales again.

"You'll definitely be a shoe-in," Patrick assures me.

"But Maya, you're really smart, I mean, like, you're the one who tells me what to write in Mr.

Jordan's class all the time, you're not my lab partner, you're like my lab answer."

"Yeah, but Dave, you won all those science fairs when you were just a freshman."

"Yeah, but, like, you've got those debate team things and that history competition, plus aren't you on varsity tennis?"

"She's number two or something," Patrick adds.

"Our problems are not real problems," Robert says very loudly into the window.

There's a silence between us, and we look at him.

None of us knows what to say.

"Do you guys remember when Mr. Jordan hit me in the head that one time?" Robert says.

"Yeah," I say.

"I don't even remember what I did, I just remember him walking up to me from behind his desk and hitting me in the back of the head. It was so unreal."

There was another pause. I check the rearview mirror intermittently to see Robert. His forehead is pressed into the window so his left eyeball almost touches the glass. His mouth is slacked open and I can't tell if he's smiling or grimacing.

"I hate chemistry," Patrick says.

"But didn't you get a 5 on the AP test?" Maya asks.

"Yeah, he got a 5," I say, growling a little bit.

"What'd you get?" Maya asks.

"I got a 4."

"But you're not a math person, Dave," she assures me.

"And you are?"

"I always did well in math," she says.

"I hate math," Patrick says, "I always get B's."

"I guess I'm more of an English person," I say.

"Yeah, you are. You can write," Maya says.

"I don't know what kind of person I am," Patrick says.

Robert snorts and laughs when Patrick says this. I look back at him, and his face is still pressed up against the glass. He doesn't stop laughing.

Why does he laugh?

After he woke up screaming, Robert said his nose bled and that he passed out and woke up in the hospital. I asked him why he thought all that happened, and he said he didn't know. He said his parents took him to his doctor back in Danbury, and the doctor said he was in great shape, that he was a "healthy young man." He doesn't smoke. He gets exercise. He doesn't drink. He said:

"My stomach felt like it was crashing in, like there was this tightening, like had I had to go to the bathroom. I got hot chills up and down my arms and I started having trouble breathing, like my chest hurt, stung in the middle. Then I started crying because it hurt so much and I passed out. I woke up on my side in the hospital and someone was looking at my butt or something and my eyes were heavy like I was still crying. My parents were there and I passed out again and then I woke up and no one was there, I was still behind the curtain, but I felt fine, like nothing was wrong. I was tired and my stomach felt empty. But I was okay."

I asked him if anything had happened since then.

"No," he said. "Not at all. No one could figure it out. The doctors said I was healthy. They said everything was fine. That there wasn't anything wrong with me. My parents looked scared and asked me all the time how I was, they still do, but I feel fine. Well, not totally fine. I feel a little scared sometimes that it'll happen again, like I'm just sitting there and wham! I'm terrified and can't breathe. But it's been like a week and I'm okay."

I asked him why he thought this happened to him.

"I don't know, I mean, we're expected to be so much and do so much. We're supposed to take the tests and study and do these internships get into college and go to college and no one really cares why. No one asks. No one thinks. We're expected to be impressive for the sake of being impressive, so other people will think we're great and think our parents are great. That's what we are, we're the Impressives. But why?"

Maya's dad helped us set up a venue near the capitol building. Patrick's dad got permission from the city. My mom and dad helped get the word out to friends and paid for fliers. Robert's parents found a company that would take the Pathfinder away after it got destroyed.

We make it past Baltimore and we're going through a tunnel that our Internet directions say will get us to D.C. The fluorescent lights inside the tunnel are over us and we drive in a steady stream of cars going about sixty miles an hour.

"What are we doing?" Roberts asks the window.

We all look at one another.

"We're going to help people," I say.

Then my stomach clenches, it tightens, and I feel a stinging in the middle of my chest and my throat closes and it feels like my arms are asleep and I can't breathe and the last thing I see is the wall of the tunnel, dark and electric yellow, coming at us and my friends screaming and then nothing.

Why did this happen to us?

Because we're the Impressives.

A Manual for Readers

"Rejoice."
–Donald Barthelme, from *The Dead Father*

INDEX
first-person
second-person
third-person
long-thin
twitter-sized
square
with many paragraph breaks
with rhetorical questions
long
by a famous person
by an unknown person

First-person stories are fraught with scars
shaped like "I". These scars occur in every
sentence. They've been in fights with bears,
manually-operated lawnmowers, and women
with pedicures. To soothe them, replace each of
their I-shaped scars with a palliative "it" and
reread twice thusly. They will complain at first.

Just wait. They will thank you at the end of the second reading.

Second-person stories are very demanding of "you." They demand that "you" take out the trash, "you" have intercourse with your cousin, "you" kill a lover in a cave, etc. Second-person stories will tell you what to do, but they mean to take you by the hand and leadeth you through green pastures, yea, though you walk through the valley of the shadow of death, you shall fear no evil for they art with "you," amen.

Third-person stories, as their name connotes, don't need you or anyone else. They're fine just by themselves. They get persnickety, though, when they overhear questions being put to their omniscient narrators who, like the Wizard of Oz, are wonderful in some ways but snivelish in others. If you find the Wizard of a third-person story she will try to seem bigger than she is by casting turquoise images to obfuscate. Don't be fooled: she wants you to slide the silk curtain away and let the sunlight hit her. She wants to be seen through, though she's done a thorough job hiding herself.

The long-thin story is a story of dialogue between two synchronized personalities tuned like piano strings in a writer's mind. They discuss war, windmills, menstrual cycles, police reports, and mysterious disappearances. They may talk on the phone or in the parlor or in a truck parked in a parking lot in the town where they grew up. The dialogue stretches down the page like a tape worm seeking refuge. Therefore, to remove the long-thin story, a cracker must be held at the opening of the mouth after five days of fasting to entice it to crawl up the esophagus. The story will starve. It will crawl up your throat to get the cracker. When it takes the bait, grab it by its title and pull it up and out of you.

The twitter-sized story says more or less what she is and is more or less than she says. She blurps, spurts, then silent-farts her narrative, which escapes into the air through a blow hole on her smooth back. The twitter-sized story must be consumed like popcorn, that relatively recent snack made from the ancient strain of budding plant (maize) that was grown and harvested, we must remember, in the times of Gilgamesh, when the first twitter-sized stories were written.

The square story swims in front of you like a blowfish. He demands your attention for a slightly longer period than the twitter story, but with the intention of showing you to yourself in the manner of the ever-so-brief. (This is different than the never-so-brief and the always-so-brief.) The square story is shaped like a frame of consciousness in the tradition of the pictorial theory of meaning, wherein a proposition is a picture that depicts a state of affairs. Accordingly, the square story may be framed and put on the mantel next to the picture of your three beautiful Schnauzers, whom you tell apart by their differently-colored handkerchiefs. The square story's personality may vary in just this way.

The story with many paragraph breaks wants you to look at each of its parts. It is a Ford Model T that has suddenly taken on the soul of Woody Allen after Allen's unexpected passing. It hiccups what it believes are well-constructed phrases and dialogue and description. The writer of the story with many paragraph breaks has fiddled with the format of the text in their word processing program such that they've processed the words in every way and have decided that, like doting parents of spoiled children, each sentence must be seen in the light of its own shining quality, which is obviously present.

The story with rhetorical questions is an impostor-sophist, a lawyer-story. Don't believe it. Don't look at it another second. It doesn't understand itself. This is why it asks itself questions that it already knows the answers to. Calmly ask it to be still and wash its hair with a lice shampoo. Comb out the questions like parasites from the story's curly locks with the understanding that parasites were created (by god or the random walk of evolution over natural selection or plasma-based aliens) to be what they are. They cannot help it. They are honestly parasitic. For this reason stories with rhetorical questions must be sung to with lullabies just before they're flushed down the toilet.

The long story is an incredible blob that wants to take you into it's jellied folds and keep you there until it spits out a better version of you. It thinks itself a giver of worthy gifts. Give it the benefit of the doubt. It is excited to see you, small though you are in its eyes. This may seem belittling. It is. But we all must be belittled at one time or another, and the onus is on the small if giants are to be conquered. Allow yourself to be surrounded by the blob of the long story. It will be uncomfortable at first–the first sensations of a blob will always demand fast adaptation–but once you sink in and trust it you'll see its gifts and you'll exit with new patiences. These patiences will help you achieve your goals, no matter they are.

The story written by a famous person has all the advantages. It has wealthy parents in a capitalist system. It has perfect teeth. It hangs out with the cool kids. It has all the clothes from all the commercials. It starred in the commercials. It is accepted as a genius by the department when it is still an undergraduate and is given a doctorate by the chair of the department. Pay attention to this story, but do so quietly. Watch it like the nerd watches the jock. Watch it like Heraclitus next to a river, repeating word "flux" yourself. Know that the story by a famous person suffers inside, just like you; that it is small and juvenile, just like you; that it has not asked to be what everyone supposes it is, just like you; that the material world is a world of hierarchy-makers whose gazes have just so happened to fall upon it; that its immaterial nature, its soul, is just as fragile as yours. The functions of celebrity over time have forced this lipstick upon it. But every story by a famous person knows that the roots of its fame are buried deep in the dirt. Listen, they are constantly begging with their birdsongs to be treated like everyone else.

The story by an unknown person is standing by himself in a convention center. Everyone around him talks while he talks. He has traveled from South Dakota to be here, packed his big green suitcase. He has had his suit hemmed. He has purchased cologne and has used it. He has left his wife and child, who are beautiful and love him dearly, to attend this convention. His hopes are high and his confidence at the breaking point. He speaks as convention-goers pass his table by, looking at the bright displays of the stories by famous people. He sweats, wondering why he has come. He castigates himself and begins to think he should pack up and go, but the story from an unknown person continues talking, deluded by the dream he's dreamed for so long in his sleepless nights: that someone will hear him, will find a melody in his voice, just as he has found melodies in the voices of others. If you are attending the convention, keep this story in mind, look for him–you will recognize his blue-green eyes and wavy hair. On your way to the big show, stop for him and smile and listen. Everybody wins in this.